Alice's Adventures Under Ground

ALICE'S ADVENTURES
UNDER GROUND

BY LEWIS CARROLL

Facsimile of the author's manuscript book
with additional material from the
facsimile edition of 1886

With a New Introduction by Martin Gardner

DOVER PUBLICATIONS, INC.
NEW YORK

Copyright © 1965 by Dover Publications, Inc.

All rights reserved under Pan American and International Copyright Conventions.

Published in Canada by General Publishing Company, Ltd., 30 Lesmill Road, Don Mills, Toronto, Ontario.

Published in the United Kingdom by Constable and Company, Ltd., 10 Orange Street, London WC 2.

This new Dover edition, first published in 1965, has been made from photographs of the Lewis Carroll manuscript in the possession of the British Museum. It also contains material from the facsimile edition published by Macmillan & Co., Ltd., in London in 1886. Martin Gardner has written a new Introduction especially for this Dover edition.

Library of Congress Catalog Card Number: 65-27014

Manufactured in the United States of America

Dover Publications, Inc.
180 Varick Street
New York, N. Y. 10014

INTRODUCTION TO DOVER EDITION

It is not widely known that the Reverend Charles Lutwidge Dodgson, better known as Lewis Carroll, wrote three, possibly four, quite different versions of *Alice's Adventures in Wonderland.*

It all began on July 4, 1862. That was the "golden afternoon" on which Carroll and his friend Robinson Duckworth took three little girls on a boating trip up the Isis, a tributary of the Thames. The girls were the daughters of Henry George Liddell (his name rhymed with "fiddle"), dean of Christ Church, Oxford, where Carroll taught mathematics. Carroll was especially fond of Alice Liddell, then ten. It was mainly for her that he began his story of another Alice's tumble down the rabbit hole, inventing the whimsical details as he went along.

The "interminable fairy-tale," as Carroll referred to it in his diary, lasted through many later boating trips. Carroll assured Alice that he would write it all down for her, but it was not until February of the following year that the task was completed. This first manuscript, which he called *Alice's Adventures under Ground,* was probably destroyed by Carroll in 1864 when he prepared a more elaborate hand-printed copy with thirty-seven pictures drawn by himself. We cannot be sure, but it seems likely that this second manuscript differed in many respects from the first. At any rate, we do know that on November 26, 1864, Carroll gave it to Alice as a Christmas present.

While Carroll was preparing this second version of his story, friends were urging him to find a publisher for it. He set about revising and expanding until the story was almost twice as long as it had been, and considerably more sophisticated. It was published by Macmillan and Company, in London, with illustrations by John Tenniel, on July 4, 1865. Carroll had suggested the date to commemorate the day, three years earlier, on which he had first extemporized his story.

The fourth and final version of *Alice* was a complete rewriting of the tale for very young children — children "from nought to five," as Carroll put it in his preface. This was brought out by

Macmillan in 1889 with twenty of Tenniel's pictures enlarged and colored. (It is amusing to learn that Carroll rejected the first printing because the colors were too gaudy; the books were then offered to a New York publisher who refused them on the grounds that the colors were too dull.)

The volume now in the reader's hands is a facsimile of the second manuscript, exactly as Carroll hand-lettered and illustrated it for Alice Liddell. In March, 1885, Carroll obtained Alice's permission (she was then Mrs. Hargreaves) to allow Macmillan to issue the first facsimile of this manuscript. It went on sale on December 22 of the following year, in an edition of 5,000 copies. On the last page of his original manuscript Carroll had pasted a small oval photograph of Alice, taken when she was seven, the age of Alice in the story. The upper part of this oval had separated the story's last two words. Because the photograph was removed from Macmillan's 1886 facsimile, the final line had to be relettered to close the gap.

Stuart Dodgson Collingwood, in his *Life and Letters of Lewis Carroll*, prints two letters from Carroll to Alice: one dated March 1, 1885, requesting her permission to publish the facsimile; the other, dated November 11, 1886, reporting his progress in preparing this edition. Both letters are so characteristic of Carroll, so revealing of his fondness for Alice Liddell, and so filled with interesting details about the history of the first facsimile, that they are worth quoting in full:

> My dear Mrs. Hargreaves:
>
> I fancy this will come to you almost like a voice from the dead, after so many years of silence, and yet those years have made no difference that I can perceive in *my* clearness of memory of the days when we *did* correspond. I am getting to feel what an old man's[1] failing memory is as to recent events and new friends, (for instance, I made friends, only a few weeks ago, with a very nice little maid of about twelve, and had a walk with her—and now I can't recall either of her names!), but my mental picture is as vivid as ever of one who was, through so many years, my ideal child-friend.

---

[1] Carroll was then fifty-three.

I have had scores of child-friends since your time, but they have been quite a different thing.

However, I did not begin this letter to say all *that*. What I want to ask is, Would you have any objection to the original MS. book of "Alice's Adventures" (which I suppose you still possess) being published in facsimile? The idea of doing so occurred to me only the other day. If, on consideration, you come to the conclusion that you would rather *not* have it done, there is an end of the matter. If, however, you give a favourable reply, I would be much obliged if you would lend it me (registered post, I should think, would be safest) that I may consider the possibilities. I have not seen it for about twenty years, so am by no means sure that the illustrations may not prove to be so awfully bad that to reproduce them would be absurd.

There can be no doubt that I should incur the charge of gross egoism in publishing it. But I don't care for that in the least, knowing that I have no such motive; only I think, considering the extraordinary popularity the books have had (we have sold more than 120,000 of the two), there must be many who would like to see the original form.

Always your friend,
C. L. Dodgson.

My dear Mrs. Hargreaves:

Many thanks for your permission to insert "Hospitals" in the Preface to your book.[2] I have had almost as many adventures in getting that unfortunate facsimile finished, *Above* ground, as your namesake had *Under* it!

First, the zincographer in London, recommended to me for photographing the book, page by page, and preparing the zinc-blocks, declined to undertake it unless I would entrust the book to *him,* which I entirely refused to do. I felt that it was only due to you, in return for your great kindness in lending so unique a book, to be scrupulous in not letting it be even *touched* by the workmen's hands. In vain I offered to come and reside in London with the book, and to attend daily in the studio, to place it in position to be photographed, and turn over the pages as required. He said that could not be done because "other authors' works were being photographed there, which must on no

---

[2] A reference to the postscript of the preface.

account be seen by the public." I undertook not to look at *anything* but my own book; but it was no use: we could not come to terms.

Then —— recommended me a certain Mr. X——,[3] an excellent photographer, but in so small a way of business that I should have to *prepay* him, bit by bit, for the zinc-blocks: and *he* was willing to come to Oxford, and do it here. So it was all done in my studio, I remaining in waiting all the time, to turn over the pages.

But I daresay I have told you so much of the story already.

Mr. X—— did a first-rate set of negatives, and took them away with him to get the zinc-blocks made. These he delivered pretty regularly at first, and there seemed to be every prospect of getting the book out by Christmas, 1885.

On October 18, 1885, I sent your book to Mrs. Liddell, who had told me your sisters were going to visit you and would take it with them. I trust it reached you safely?

Soon after this—I having prepaid for the whole of the zinc-blocks—the supply suddenly ceased, while twenty-two pages were still due, and Mr. X—— disappeared!

My belief is that he was in hiding from his creditors. We sought him in vain. So things went on for months. At one time I thought of employing a detective to find him, but was assured that "all detectives are scoundrels." The alternative seemed to be to ask you to lend the book again, and get the missing pages re-photographed. But I was most unwilling to rob you of it again, and also afraid of the risk of loss of the book, if sent by post—for even "registered post" does not seem *absolutely* safe.

In April he called at Macmillan's and left *eight* blocks, and again vanished into obscurity.

This left us with fourteen pages (dotted up and down the book) still missing. I waited awhile longer, and then put the thing into the hands of a solicitor, who soon found the man, but could get nothing but promises from him. "You will never get the blocks," said the solicitor, "unless you frighten him by a summons before a magistrate." To this at last I unwillingly consented: the summons had to be taken out at —— (that is where this aggravating man is living), and this entailed two journeys from Eastbourne—

---

[3] A Mr. Noad, as we learn from Carroll's diary.

one to get the summons (my *personal* presence being necessary), and the other to attend in court with the solicitor on the day fixed for hearing the case. The defendant didn't appear; so the magistrate said he would take the case in his absence. Then I had the new and exciting experience of being put into the witness-box, and sworn, and cross-examined by a rather savage magistrate's clerk, who seemed to think that, if he only bullied me enough, he would soon catch me out in a falsehood! I had to give the magistrate a little lecture on photo-zincography, and the poor man declared the case was so complicated he must adjourn it for another week. But this time, in order to secure the presence of our slippery defendant, he issued a warrant for his apprehension, and the constable had orders to take him into custody and lodge him in prison, the night before the day when the case was to come on. The news of *this* effectually frightened him, and he delivered up the fourteen negatives (he hadn't done the blocks) before the fatal day arrived. I was rejoiced to get them, even though it entailed the paying a second time for getting the fourteen blocks done, and withdrew the action.

The fourteen blocks were quickly done and put into the printer's hands; and all is going on smoothly at last: and I quite hope to have the book completed, and to be able to send you a very special copy (bound in white vellum, unless you would prefer some other style of binding) by the end of the month.

Believe me always,
Sincerely yours,
C. L. Dodgson.

The original manuscript of *Alice's Adventures under Ground* was sold in April, 1928, to A. S. W. Rosenbach, of Philadelphia, who resold it six months later to Eldridge R. Johnson, of Moorestown, New Jersey. According to Warren Weaver, who gives these details in his book *Alice in Many Tongues* (University of Wisconsin Press, 1964), after Johnson's death the manuscript was sold back to Rosenbach in 1946 for $50,000. Luther H. Evans, then Librarian of Congress, felt strongly that the manuscript belonged in England. He persuaded Rosenbach to sell it again (after raising $50,000 from various persons), and in 1948

Evans gave it to the British Museum where it remains today. Weaver quotes the Archbishop of Canterbury, who accepted the gift for the Museum, as saying that its return to England was "an unsullied and innocent act in a distracted and sinful world."

Several facsimiles have been published in the United States. The present Dover facsimile was prepared with the cooperation of the British Museum, directly from photographs of the original manuscript. Carroll's title and dedication pages are reproduced in their original color on the front and back covers of this edition, though the colors he gave to initial letters of chapter headings could not be shown. The book is accurate in every respect, including the photograph of Alice, still attached to the final page of the original.

In addition to Carroll's manuscript book, this edition contains the following material, reproduced from the Macmillan 1886 facsimile: Carroll's preface, his "Easter Greeting," his poem called "Christmas Greetings," and the book's two pages of advertising. These, with the exception of the preface, appeared at the end of the Macmillan volume. The design facing the Dover title page is that which appeared on the binding of the 1886 Macmillan facsimile.

It is difficult today to read Carroll's preface and "Easter Greeting" without embarrassment. "No shadow of sin," indeed! One wonders how he would have explained a battle between two rival siblings over, say, who gets the last cookie in the jar. "Innocent laughter" and "merry voices" as youngsters "roll among the hay"? Carroll has a point, but it is so plastered over with what H. L. Mencken liked to call "pious piffle," and with rationalizations for his abnormal devotion to little girls, that I suspect even the most devout Victorians shuddered a bit as they read.

Many of Carroll's changes, when he revised this story for its first book publication, consisted of the addition of entirely new characters, new episodes, and new poems. The Mad Tea Party and the Pig and Pepper chapters were added. The trial of the Knave of Hearts was enlarged from the less than two pages it occupies here to two new chapters. Neither the Cheshire Cat nor the Ugly Duchess is in the original, though there is a briefly mentioned Marchioness who later turns out to be the Queen. That famous shaped poem, the Mouse's Tail, is completely different here (p. 28).[4] The episode on pages 26 and 27, in which the Dodo leads everyone to a cottage to get dry, recalls an occasion in 1862 when Dodgson and Duckworth (the Dodo and the Duck) and the three Liddell girls, had actually been caught in a downpour during another boating trip. Carroll had led the group (it also included two of Carroll's sisters and his aunt Lucy: the "several other curious creatures" mentioned on p. 22) to a friend's home where they dried their clothes. Carroll assumed this incident would be of little interest outside the small circle of those involved, so he took it out and substituted the story of the Caucus Race.

Carroll also later removed, from pages 14 and 15, the names of Gertrude and Florence. They were probably friends or relatives of Alice, and since the references to Florence were unkind, he changed the names to Ada and Mabel. Knowledgeable readers will spot other details in which the manuscript differs from the familiar version: the White Rabbit's nosegay (p. 13) that later became a fan, the Caterpillar's distinction between the mushroom's top and stalk (p. 61) that later became a distinction between right and left sides, the ostrich (p. 76) that became a flamingo, and so on.

No one knows whether Tenniel saw Carroll's drawings before he made his own sketches. There are obvious similarities here and there, but some such resemblances would have been hard to avoid. Carroll was not much of an artist, as he himself was fully aware, but his illustrations are nonetheless fascinating. They show, more accurately than Tenniel's drawings, how Carroll imagined his curious characters. And there are amusing details, such as the kissing courtiers on page 75 and some not consciously intended aspects of special interest to Freudian symbol searchers, that call for more than a casual inspection of the pictures.

MARTIN GARDNER

Hastings-on-Hudson, New York
July, 1965

---

[4]Page references are to the clearer set of numbers, running from 1 to 90, found in the upper outside corner of each page; these correspond to the page numbers of the Macmillan 1886 edition. The other set of numbers, running from 1 to 47, refers to folios in the British Museum manuscript.

CONTENTS

Complete facsimile of the British Museum manuscript
of *Alice's Adventures under Ground*

Front matter of the Macmillan 1886 edition
 Title page
 Printer's identification
 Carroll's preface ("Who will Riddle me . . .")
 Postscript to Carroll's preface
 Contents page

Back matter of the Macmillan 1886 edition
 An Easter Greeting . . .
 Christmas Greetings
 List of Carroll's works then published by Macmillan

Chapter 1.

Alice was beginning to get very tired of sitting by her sister on the bank, and of having nothing to do: once or twice she had peeped into the book her sister was reading, but it had no pictures or conversations in it, and where is the use of a book, thought Alice, without pictures or conversations? So she was considering in her own mind, (as well as she could, for the hot day made her feel very sleepy and stupid,) whether the pleasure of making a daisy-chain was worth the trouble of getting up and picking the daisies, when a white rabbit with pink eyes ran close by her.

There was nothing very remarkable in that, nor did Alice think it so very much out of the way to hear the rabbit say to itself "dear, dear! I shall be too late!" (when she thought it over afterwards, it occurred to her that she ought to have wondered at this, but at the time it all seemed quite natural); but when the rabbit actually took a watch out of its waistcoat-pocket, looked at it, and then hurried on, Alice started to her feet, for it flashed across her mind that she had never before seen a rabbit with either a waistcoat-pocket or a watch to take out of it, and, full of curiosity, she hurried across the field after it, and was just in time to see it pop down a large rabbit-hole under the hedge. In a moment down went Alice after it, never once considering how in the world she was to get out again.

The rabbit-hole went straight on like a tunnel for some way, and then dipped suddenly down, so suddenly, that Alice had not a moment to think about stopping herself, before she found herself falling down what seemed a deep well. Either the well was very deep, or she fell very slowly, for she had plenty of time as she went down to look about her, and to wonder what would happen next. First, she tried to look down and make out what she was coming to, but it was too dark to see anything: then, she looked at the sides of the well, and noticed that they were filled with cupboards and book--shelves; here and there were maps and pictures hung on pegs. She took a jar down off one of of the shelves as she passed: it was labelled

"Orange Marmalade", but to her great disappointment it was empty: she did not like to drop the jar, for fear of killing somebody underneath, so managed to put it into one of the cupboards as she fell past it.

"Well!" thought Alice to herself, "after such a fall as this, I shall think nothing of tumbling down stairs! How brave they'll all think me at home! Why, I wouldn't say anything about it, even if I fell off the top of the house!" (which was most likely true.)

Down, down, down. Would the fall _never_ come to an end? "I wonder how many miles I've fallen by this time?" said she aloud, "I must be getting somewhere near the centre of the earth. Let me see: that would be four thousand miles down, I think —" (for you see Alice had learnt several things of this sort in her lessons in the schoolroom, and though this was not a _very_ good opportunity of showing off her knowledge, as there was no one to hear her, still it was good practice to say it over,) "yes, that's the right distance, but then what Longitude or Latitude-line shall I be in?" (Alice had no idea what Longitude was, or Latitude either, but she thought they were nice grand words to say.)

Presently she began again: "I wonder if I shall fall right <u>through</u> the earth! How funny it'll be to come out among the people that walk with their heads downwards! But I shall have to ask them what the name of the country is, you know. Please, Ma'am, is this New Zealand or Australia?"— and she tried to curtsey as she spoke, (fancy <u>curtseying</u> as you're falling through the air! do you think you could manage it?) "and what an ignorant little girl she'll think me for asking! No, it'll never do to ask: perhaps I shall see it written up somewhere."

Down, down, down: there was nothing else to do, so Alice soon began talking again. "Dinah will miss me very much tonight, I should think!" (Dinah was the cat.) "I hope they'll remember her saucer of milk at tea-time! Oh, dear Dinah, I wish I had you here! There are no mice in the air, I'm afraid, but you might catch a bat, and that's very like a mouse, you know, my dear. But do cats eat bats, I wonder?" And here Alice began to get rather sleepy, and kept on saying to herself, in a dreamy sort of way "do cats eat bats? do cats eat bats?" and sometimes, "do bats eat cats?" for, as she couldn't answer either question, it didn't much matter which way she put it. She felt that she was dozing off, and had just begun to dream that she was walking hand in hand with Dinah, and was saying to her very earnestly, "Now, Dinah, my dear, tell me the truth. Did you ever eat a bat?" when suddenly, bump! bump! down she came upon a heap of sticks and shavings, and the fall was over.

Alice was not a bit hurt, and jumped on to her feet directly: she looked up, but it was all dark overhead; before her was another long passage, and the white rabbit was still in sight, hurrying down it. There was not a moment to be lost: away went Alice like the wind, and just heard it say, as it turned a corner, "my ears and whiskers, how late it's getting!" She turned the corner after it, and instantly found herself in a long, low hall, lit up by a row of lamps which hung from the roof.

There were doors all round the hall, but they were all locked, and when Alice had been all round it, and tried them all, she walked sadly down the middle, wondering how she was ever to get out again: suddenly she came upon a little three-legged table, all made of solid glass; there was nothing lying upon it, but a tiny golden key, and Alice's first idea was that it might belong to one of the doors of the hall, but alas! either the locks were too large, or the key too small, but at any rate it would open none of them. However, on the second time round, she came to a low curtain, behind which was a door about eighteen inches high: she tried the little key in the keyhole, and it fitted! Alice opened the door, and looked down a small passage, not larger than a rat-hole, into the loveliest garden you ever saw. How she longed to get out of that dark hall, and wander about among those beds of bright flowers and those cool fountains, but she could not even get her head through the doorway, "and even if my head would go through," thought poor Alice, " it would be very little use without my shoulders. Oh, how I wish I could shut up like a telescope! I think I could, if I only knew how to begin." For, you see, so many out-of-the-way things had happened lately, that Alice began to think very few things indeed were really impossible.

There was nothing else to do, so she went back to the table, half hoping she might find another key on it, or at any rate a book of rules for shutting up people like telescopes: this time there was a little bottle on it — " which certainly was not there before" said Alice — and tied round the neck of the bottle was a paper label with the words **DRINK ME** beautifully printed on it in large letters.

It was all very well to say "drink me," "but I'll look first," said the wise little Alice, "and see whether the bottle's marked "poison" or not," for Alice had read several nice little stories about children that got burnt, and eaten up by wild beasts, and other unpleasant things, because they would not remember the simple rules their friends had given them, such as, that, if you get into the fire, it will burn you, and that, if you cut your finger very deeply with a knife, it generally bleeds, and she had never forgotten that, if you drink a bottle marked "poison", it is almost certain to disagree with you, sooner or later.

However, this bottle was *not* marked poison, so Alice tasted it, and finding it very nice, (it had, in fact, a sort of mixed flavour of cherry-tart, custard, pine-apple, roast turkey, toffy, and hot buttered toast,) she very soon finished it off.

* * * * * *

"What a curious feeling!" said Alice, "I must be shutting up like a telescope."

It was so indeed: she was now only ten inches high, and her face brightened up as it occurred to her that she was now the right size for going through the little door into that lovely garden. First, however, she waited for a few minutes to see whether she was going to shrink any further: she felt a little nervous about this, "for it might end, you know," said Alice to herself, "in my going out altogether, like a candle, and what should I be like then, I wonder?" and she tried to fancy what the flame of a candle is like after the candle is blown out, for she could not remember having ever seen one. However, nothing more happened, so she decided on going into the garden at once, but, alas for poor Alice! when she got to the door, she found she had forgotten the little golden key, and when she went back to the table for the key, she found she could not possibly reach it: she could see it plainly enough through the glass, and she tried her best to climb up one of the legs of the table, but it was too slippery, and when she had tired herself out with trying, the poor little thing sat down and cried.

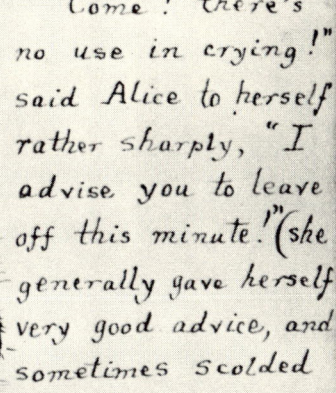

"Come! there's no use in crying!" said Alice to herself rather sharply, "I advise you to leave off this minute!" (she generally gave herself very good advice, and sometimes scolded herself so severely as to bring tears into her eyes, and once she remembered boxing her own ears for having been unkind to herself in a game of croquet she was playing with herself, for this curious child was very fond of pretending to be two people,) "but it's no use now", thought poor Alice, "to pretend to be two people! Why, there's hardly enough of me left to make one respectable person!"

Soon her eyes fell on a little ebony box lying under the table: she opened it, and found in it a very small cake, on which was lying a card with the words EAT ME beautifully printed on it in large letters. "I'll eat," said Alice, "and if it makes me larger, I can reach the key, and if it makes me smaller, I can creep under the door, so either way I'll get into the garden, and I don't care which happens!"

She eat a little bit, and said anxiously to herself "which way? which way?" and laid her hand on the top of her head to feel which way it was growing, and was quite surprised to find that she remained the same size: to be sure this is what generally happens when one eats cake, but Alice had got into the way of expecting nothing but out- -of-the way things to happen, and it seemed quite dull and stupid for things to go on in the common way.

So she set to work, and very soon finished off the cake.

* * * * *

"Curiouser and curiouser!" cried Alice, (she was so surprised that she quite forgot how to speak good English,) "now I'm opening out like the largest telescope that ever was! Goodbye, feet!" (for when she looked down at her feet, they seemed almost out of sight, they were getting so far off,) "oh, my poor little feet, I wonder who will put on your shoes and stockings for you now, dears? I'm sure I ca'n't! I shall be a great deal too far off to bother myself about you: you must manage the best way you can— but I must be kind to them", thought Alice, "or perhaps they won't walk the way I want to go! Let me see: I'll give them a new pair of boots every Christmas."

And she went on planning to herself how she would manage it

"they must go by the carrier," she thought, "and how funny it'll seem, sending presents to one's own feet! And how odd the directions will look! ALICE'S RIGHT FOOT, ESQ.
THE CARPET,
with ALICE'S LOVE
oh dear! what nonsense I am talking!"

Just at this moment, her head struck against the roof of the hall: in fact, she was now rather more than nine feet high, and she at once took up the little golden key, and hurried off to the garden door.

Poor Alice! it was as much as she could do, lying down on one side, to look through into the garden with one eye, but to get through was more hopeless than ever: she sat down and cried again.

"You ought to be ashamed of yourself," said Alice, "a great girl like you," (she might well say this,) "to cry in this way! Stop this instant, I tell you!" But she cried on all the same, shedding gallons of tears, until there was a large pool, about four inches deep, all round her, and reaching half way across the hall. After a time, she heard a little pattering of feet in the distance, and

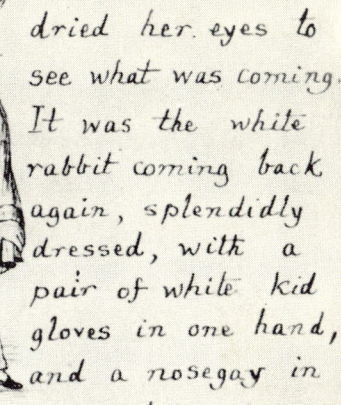
dried her eyes to see what was coming. It was the white rabbit coming back again, splendidly dressed, with a pair of white kid gloves in one hand, and a nosegay in the other. Alice was ready to ask help of any one, she felt so desperate, and as the rabbit passed her, she said, in a low, timid voice, "If you please, Sir ⎯⎯ " the rabbit started violently, looked up once into the roof of the hall, from which the voice seemed to come, and then dropped the nosegay and the white kid gloves, and skurried away into the darkness as hard as it could go.

Alice took up the nosegay and gloves, and found the nosegay so delicious that she kept smelling at it all the time she went on talking to herself ⎯⎯ "dear, dear! how queer everything is today! and yesterday everything happened just as usual: I wonder if I was changed in the night? Let me think: was I the same when I got up this morning? I think I remember feeling rather different. But if I'm not the same, who in the world am I? Ah, that's the great puzzle!" And she began thinking over all the children she knew of the same age as herself, to see if she could have been changed for any of them.

"I'm sure I'm not Gertrude," she said, "for her hair goes in such long ringlets, and mine doesn't go in ringlets at all — and I'm sure I can't be Florence, for I know all sorts of things, and she, oh! she knows such a very little! Besides, she's she, and I'm I, and — oh dear! how puzzling it all is! I'll try if I know all the things I used to know. Let me see: four times five is twelve, and four times six is thirteen, and four times seven is fourteen — oh dear! I shall never get to twenty at this rate! But the Multiplication Table don't signify — let's try Geography. London is the capital of France, and Rome is the capital of Yorkshire, and Paris — oh dear! dear! that's all wrong, I'm certain! I must have been changed for Florence! I'll try and say "How doth the little"," and she crossed her hands on her

lap, and began, but her voice sounded
hoarse and strange, and the words did not
sound the same as they used to do:

"How doth the little crocodile
　　Improve its shining tail,
And pour the waters of the Nile
　　On every golden scale!

How cheerfully it seems to grin!
　　How neatly spreads its claws!
And welcomes little fishes in
　　With gently-smiling jaws!"

"I'm sure those are not the right
words", said poor Alice, and her eyes filled
with tears as she thought "I must be
Florence after all, and I shall have to go and
live in that poky little house, and have
next to no toys to play with, and oh! ever
so many lessons to learn! No! I've made
up my mind about it: if I'm Florence,
I'll stay down here! It'll be no use their
putting their heads down and saying 'come
up, dear!' I shall only look up and say

'who am I, then? answer me that first, and then, if I like being that person, I'll come up: if not, I'll stay down here till I'm somebody else —— but, oh dear!" cried Alice with a sudden burst of tears, "I do wish they would put their heads down! I am so tired of being all alone here!"

As she said this, she looked down at her hands, and was surprised to find she had put on one of the rabbit's little gloves while she was talking. "How can I have done that?" thought she, "I must be growing small again." She got up and went to the table to measure herself by it, and found that, as nearly as she could guess, she was now about two feet high, and was going on shrinking rapidly: soon she found out that the reason of it was the nosegay she held in her hand: she dropped it hastily, just in time to save herself from shrinking away altogether, and found that she was now only three inches high.

"Now for the garden!" cried Alice,

as she hurried back to the little door, but the little door was locked again, and the little gold key was lying on the glass table as before, and "things are worse than ever!" thought the poor little girl, "for I never was as small as this before, never! And I declare it's too bad, it is!"

At this moment her foot slipped, and splash! she was up to her chin in salt water. Her first idea was that she had fallen into the sea: then she remembered that she was under ground, and she soon made out that it was the pool of tears she had wept when she was nine feet high. "I wish I hadn't cried so much!" said Alice, as she swam about, trying to find her way out, "I shall be punished for it now, I suppose, by being drowned in my own tears! Well! that'll be a queer thing, to be sure! However, every thing is queer today." Very soon she saw something splashing about in the pool near her: at first she thought it must be a walrus or a hippopotamus, but then she remembered how small she was herself, and soon made out that it was only a mouse, that had slipped in like herself.

"Would it be any use, now," thought Alice, "to speak to this mouse? The rabbit is something quite out-of-the-way, no doubt, and so have I been, ever since I came down here, but that is no reason why the mouse should not be able to talk. I think I may as well try."

So she began: "oh Mouse, do you know how to get out of this pool? I am very tired of swimming about here, oh Mouse!" The mouse looked at her rather inquisitively, and seemed to her to wink with one of its little eyes, but it said nothing.

"Perhaps it doesn't understand English," thought Alice; "I daresay it's a French mouse, come over with William the Conqueror!" (for,

19

with all her knowledge of history, Alice had no very clear notion how long ago anything had happened,) so she began again: "où est "ma chatte?" which was the first sentence out of her French lesson-book. The mouse gave a sudden jump in the pool, and seemed to quiver with fright: "oh, I beg your pardon!" cried Alice hastily, afraid that she had hurt the poor animal's feelings, "I quite forgot "you didn't like cats!"

"Not like cats!" cried the mouse, in a shrill, passionate voice, "would *you* like cats if you were me?"

"Well, perhaps not," said Alice in a soothing tone, "don't be angry about it. "And yet I wish I could show you our cat Dinah: I think you'd take a fancy to cats if you could only see her. She is such a dear quiet thing," said Alice, half to herself, as she swam lazily about in the pool, "she sits purring so nicely by the fire, licking her paws and washing her face: and she is such a nice soft thing to nurse, and she's such a capital one for catching mice — oh! I beg your pardon!" cried poor Alice again, for this time the mouse was bristling all over, and she felt certain that it was really offended, "have I offended you?"

"Offended indeed!" cried the mouse, who seemed to be positively trembling with rage, "our family always <u>hated</u> cats! Nasty, low, vulgar things! Don't talk to me about them any more!"

"I won't indeed!" said Alice, in a great hurry to change the conversation, "are you — are you — fond of — dogs?" The mouse did not answer, so Alice went on eagerly: "there is such a nice little dog near our house I should like to show you! A little bright-eyed terrier, you know, with oh! such long curly brown hair! And it'll fetch things when you throw them, and it'll sit up and beg for its dinner, and all sorts of things — I can't remember half of them — and it belongs to a farmer, and he says it kills all the rats and — oh dear!" said Alice sadly, "I'm afraid I've offended it again!" for the mouse was swimming away from her as hard as it could go, and making quite a commotion in the pool as it went.

So she called softly after it: "mouse dear! Do come back again, and we won't talk about cats and dogs any more, if you don't like them!" When the mouse heard this, it turned and swam slowly back to her: its face was quite pale, (with passion, Alice thought,) and it said in a trembling low voice "let's get to the shore, and then I'll tell you my history, and you'll understand why it is I hate cats and dogs."

It was high time to go, for the pool was getting quite full of birds and animals that had fallen into it. There was a Duck and a Dodo, a Lory and an Eaglet, and several other curious creatures. Alice led the way, and the whole party swam to the shore.

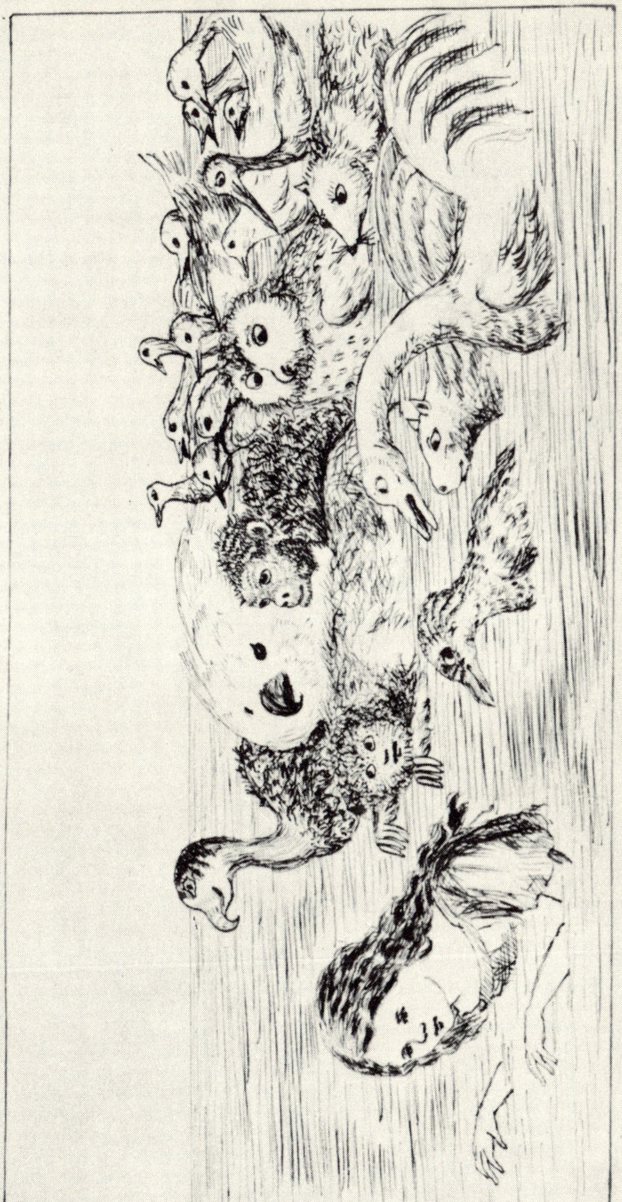

Chapter II

They were indeed a curious looking party that assembled on the bank — the birds with draggled feathers, the animals with their fur clinging close to them — all dripping wet, cross, and uncomfortable. The first question of course was, how to get dry: they had a consultation about this, and Alice hardly felt at all surprised at finding herself talking familiarly with the birds, as if she had known them all her life. Indeed, she had quite a long argument with the Lory, who at last turned sulky, and would only say "I am older than you, and must know best", and this Alice would not admit without knowing how old the Lory was, and as the Lory positively refused to tell its age, there was nothing more to be said.

At last the mouse, who seemed to have some authority among them, called out "sit down, all of you, and attend to me! I'll soon make you dry enough!" They all sat down at once, shivering, in a large ring, Alice in the middle, with her eyes anxiously fixed on the mouse, for she felt sure she would catch a bad cold if she did not get dry very soon.

"Ahem!" said the mouse, with a self-important air, "are you all ready? This is the driest thing I know. Silence all round, if you please!

"William the Conqueror, whose cause was favoured by the pope, was soon submitted to by the English, who wanted leaders, and had been of late much accustomed to usurpation and conquest. Edwin and Morcar, the earls of Mercia and Northumbria——"

"Ugh!" said the Lory with a shiver.

"I beg your pardon?" said the mouse, frowning, but very politely, "did you speak?"

"Not I!" said the Lory hastily.

"I thought you did," said the mouse, "I proceed. Edwin and Morcar, the earls of Mercia and Northumbria, declared for him;

and even Stigand, the patriotic archbishop of Canterbury, found it advisable to go with Edgar Atheling to meet William and offer him the crown. William's conduct was at first moderate — how are you getting on now, dear?" said the mouse, turning to Alice as it spoke.

"As wet as ever," said poor Alice," it doesn't seem to dry me at all."

"In that case," said the Dodo solemnly, rising to his feet," I move that the meeting adjourn, for the immediate adoption of more energetic remedies —"

"Speak English!" said the Duck," I don't know the meaning of half those long words, and what's more, I don't believe you do either!" And the Duck quacked a comfortable laugh to itself. Some of the other birds tittered audibly.

"I only meant to say," said the Dodo in a rather offended tone," that I know of a house near here, where we could get the young lady and the rest of the party dried, and then we could listen comfortably to the story which I think you were good enough to promise to tell us", bowing gravely to the mouse.

The mouse made no objection to this, and the whole party moved along the river bank, (for the pool had by this time begun to flow out of the hall, and the edge of it was fringed with rushes and forget-me-nots,) in a slow procession, the Dodo leading the way. After a time the Dodo became impatient, and, leaving the Duck to bring up the rest of the party, moved on at a quicker pace with Alice, the Lory, and the Eaglet, and soon brought them to a little cottage, and there they sat snugly by the fire, wrapped up in blankets, until the rest of the party had arrived, and they were all dry again.

Then they all sat down again in a large ring on the bank, and begged the mouse to begin his story.

"Mine is a long and a sad tale!" said the mouse, turning to Alice, and sighing.

"It *is* a long tail, certainly," said Alice, looking down with wonder at the mouse's tail, which was coiled nearly all round the party, "but why do you call it sad?" and she went on puzzling about this as the mouse went on speaking, so that her idea of the tale was something like this:

We lived beneath the mat
　Warm and snug and fat
　　But one woe, & that
　　　Was the cat!
　　　　To our joys
　　　　a clog, In
　　　our eyes a
　　fog, On our
　hearts a log
Was the dog!
　When the
cat's away,
Then
the mice
will
play,
　But, alas!
　　one day, (So they say)
　　　Came the dog and
　　　　cat, Hunting
　　　　　for a
　　　　　rat,
　　　　Crushed
　　　the mice
　　all flat,
　Each
one
as
he
sat.
　Underneath the mat, Warm & snug & fat. — Think of That!

"You are not attending!" said the mouse to Alice severely, "what are you thinking of?"

"I beg your pardon," said Alice very humbly, "you had got to the fifth bend, I think?"

"I had *not*!" cried the mouse, sharply and very angrily.

"A knot!" said Alice, always ready to make herself useful, and looking anxiously about her, "oh, do let me help to undo it!"

"I shall do nothing of the sort!" said the mouse, getting up and walking away from the party, "you insult me by talking such nonsense!".

"I didn't mean it!" pleaded poor Alice, "but you're so easily offended, you know."

The mouse only growled in reply.

"Please come back and finish your story!" Alice called after it, and the others all joined in chorus "yes, please do!" but the mouse only shook its ears, and walked quickly away, and was soon out of sight.

"What a pity it wouldn't stay!" sighed the Lory, and an old Crab took the opportunity of saying to its daughter "Ah, my dear!

let this be a lesson to you never to lose your temper!" "Hold your tongue, Ma!" said the young Crab, a little snappishly, "you're enough to try the patience of an oyster!"

"I wish I had our Dinah here, I know I do!" said Alice aloud, addressing no one in particular, "she'd soon fetch it back!"

"And who is Dinah, if I might venture to ask the question?" said the Lory.

Alice replied eagerly, for she was always ready to talk about her pet, "Dinah's our cat. And she's such a capital one for catching mice, you can't think! And oh! I wish you could see her after the birds! Why, she'll eat a little bird as soon as look at it!"

This **answer** caused a remarkable sensation among the party: some of the birds hurried off at once; one old magpie began wrapping itself up very carefully, remarking "I really must be getting home: the night air does not suit my throat," and a canary called out in a trembling voice to its children "come away from her, my dears, she's no fit company for you!" On various pretexts, they all moved off, and Alice was soon left alone.

31

She sat for some while sorrowful and silent, but she was not long before she recovered her spirits, and began talking to herself again as usual: "I do wish some of them had stayed a little longer! and I was getting to be such friends with them — really the Lory and I were almost like sisters! and so was that dear little Eaglet! And then the Duck and the Dodo! How nicely the Duck sang to us as we came along through the water: and if the Dodo hadn't known the way to that nice little cottage, I don't know when we should have got dry again——" and there is no knowing how long she might have prattled on in this way, if she had not suddenly caught the sound of pattering feet.

It was the white rabbit, trotting slowly back again, and looking anxiously about it as it went, as if it had lost something, and she heard it muttering to itself "the Marchioness! the Marchioness! oh my dear paws! oh my fur and whiskers! She'll have me executed, as sure as ferrets are ferrets! Where <u>can</u> I have dropped them, I wonder?" Alice guessed in a moment that it was looking for the nosegay and the pair of white kid gloves, and she began hunting for them, but they were now nowhere to be seen — everything seemed to have changed since her swim in the pool, and her walk along the river-bank with its fringe of rushes and forget-me-nots, and the glass table and the little door had vanished.

Soon the rabbit noticed Alice, as she stood looking curiously about her, and at once said in a quick angry tone, "why, Mary Ann! what <u>are</u> you doing out here? Go home this moment, and look on my dressing-table for my gloves and nosegay, and fetch them here, as quick as you can run, do you hear?" and Alice was so much frightened that she ran off at once, without saying a word, in the direction which the rabbit had pointed out

She soon found herself in front of a neat little house, on the door of which was a bright brass plate with the name **W. RABBIT, ESQ.** she went in, and hurried upstairs, for fear she should meet the real Mary Ann and be turned out of the house before she had found the gloves: she knew that one pair had been lost in the hall, "but of course", thought Alice, "it has plenty more of them in its house. How queer it seems to be going messages for a rabbit! I suppose Dinah'll be sending me messages next!" And she began fancying the sort of things that would happen: "Miss Alice! come here directly and get ready for your walk!" "Coming in a minute, nurse! but I've got to watch this mousehole till Dinah comes back, and see that the mouse doesnt get out——" "only I don't think," Alice went on, "that they'd let Dinah stop in the house, if it began ordering people about like that!"

By this time she had found her way into a tidy little room, with a table in the window on which was a looking-glass and, (as Alice had hoped,) two or three pairs of tiny white kid gloves: she took up a pair of gloves, and was just going to leave the room, when her eye fell upon a little bottle that stood near the looking-glass: there was no label on it this time with the words "drink me", but nevertheless she uncorked it and put it to her lips: "I know something interesting is sure to happen," she said to herself, "whenever I eat or drink anything, so I'll see what this bottle does. I do hope it'll make me grow larger, for I'm quite tired of being such a tiny little thing!"

It did so indeed, and much sooner

than she expected: before she had drunk half the bottle, she found her head pressing against the ceiling, and she stooped to save her neck from being broken, and hastily put down the bottle, saying to herself "that's quite enough — I hope I sha'n't grow any more — I wish I hadn't drunk so much!"

Alas! it was too late: she went on growing and growing, and very soon had to kneel down: in another minute there was not room even for this, and she tried the effect of lying down, with one elbow against the door, and the other arm curled round her head. Still she went on growing, and as a last resource she put one arm out of the window, and one foot up the chimney, and said to herself "now I can do no more — what will become of me?"

20 37.

Luckily for Alice, the little magic bottle had now had its full effect, and she grew no larger: still it was very uncomfortable, and, as there seemed to be no sort of chance of ever getting out of the room again, no wonder she felt unhappy. "It was much pleasanter at home," thought poor Alice, "when one wasn't always growing larger and smaller, and being ordered about by mice and rabbits — I almost wish I hadn't gone down that rabbit-hole, and yet, and yet — it's rather curious, you know, this sort of life. I do wonder what _can_ have happened to me! When I used to read fairy-tales, I fancied that sort of thing never happened, and now here I am in the middle of one! There ought to be a book written about me, that there ought! and when I grow up I'll write one — but I'm grown up now" said she in a sorrowful tone, "at least there's no room to grow up any more _here_."

"But then", thought Alice, "shall I _never_ get any older than I am now? That'll be a comfort, one way — never to be an old woman — but then — always to have lessons to learn! Oh, I shouldn't like <u>that</u>!"

"Oh, you foolish Alice!" she said again, "how can you learn lessons in here? Why, there's hardly room for you, and no room at all for any lesson-books!"

And so she went on, taking first one side, and then the other, and making quite a conversation of it altogether, but after a few minutes she heard a voice outside, which made her stop to listen.

"Mary Ann! Mary Ann!" said the voice, "fetch me my gloves this moment!" Then came a little pattering of feet on the stairs: Alice knew it was the rabbit coming to look for her, and she trembled till she shook the house, quite forgetting that she was now about a thousand times as large as the rabbit, and had no reason to be afraid of it. Presently the rabbit came to the door, and tried to open it, but as it opened inwards, and Alice's elbow was against it, the attempt proved a failure. Alice heard it say to itself "then I'll go round and get in at the window."

"*That* you won't!" thought Alice, and, after waiting till she fancied she heard the rabbit just under the window, she suddenly spread out her hand, and made a snatch in the air. She did not get hold of anything, but she heard a little shriek and a fall and a crash of breaking glass, from which she concluded that it was just possible it had fallen into a cucumber-frame, or something of the sort.

Next came an angry voice — the rabbit's — "Pat, Pat! where are you?" And then a voice she had never heard before, "shure then I'm here! digging for apples, anyway, yer honour!"

"Digging for apples indeed!" said the rabbit angrily, "here, come and help me out of this!"—Sound of more breaking glass.

"Now, tell me, Pat, what is that coming out of the window?"

"Shure it's an arm, yer honour!" (He pronounced it "arrum".)

"An arm, you goose! Who ever saw an arm that size? Why, it fills the whole window, don't you see?"

"Shure, it does, yer honour, but it's an arm for all that."

"Well, it's no business there: go and take it away!"

There was a long silence after this, and Alice could only hear whispers now and then, such as "shure I don't like it, yer honour, at all at all!" "do as I tell you, you coward!" and at last she spread out her hand again and made another snatch in the air. This time there were two little shrieks, and more breaking glass—"what a number of cucumber-frames there must be!" thought Alice, "I wonder what they'll do next! As for pulling me out of the window, I only wish they could! I'm sure I don't want to stop in here any longer!"

She waited for some time without

hearing anything more: at last came a rumbling of little cart-wheels, and the sound of a good many voices all talking together: she made out the words "where's the other ladder? — why, I hadn't to bring but one, Bill's got the other — here, put 'em up at this corner — no, tie 'em together first — they don't reach high enough yet — oh, they'll do well enough, don't be particular — here, Bill! catch hold of this rope — will the roof bear? — mind that loose slate — oh, it's coming down! heads below!—" (a loud crash) "now, who did that? — it was Bill, I fancy — who's to go down the chimney? — nay, I shan't! you do it! — that I won't then — Bill's got to go down — here, Bill! the master says you've to go down the chimney!"

"Oh, so Bill's got to come down the chimney, has he?" said Alice to herself, "why, they seem to put everything upon Bill! I wouldn't be in Bill's place for a good deal: the fireplace is a pretty tight one, but I think I can kick a little!"

She drew her foot as far down the chimney as she could, and waited till she heard a little animal (she couldn't guess what sort it was) scratching and scrambling in the chimney close above her: then, saying to herself "this is Bill", she gave one sharp kick, and waited again to see what would happen next.

The first thing was a general chorus of "there goes Bill!" then the rabbit's voice alone, "catch him, you by the hedge!" then silence, and then another confusion of voices, "how was it, old fellow? what happened to you? tell us all about it."

Last came a little feeble squeaking voice, ("that's Bill" thought Alice,) which said "well, I hardly know — I'm all of a fluster myself — something comes at me like a Jack-in-the-box, and the next minute up I goes like a rocket!" "And so you did, old fellow!" said the other voices.

"We must burn the house down!" said the voice of the rabbit, and Alice called out as loud as she could "if you do, I'll set Dinah at you!" This caused silence again, and while Alice was thinking "but how can I get Dinah here?" she found to her great delight that she was getting smaller: very soon she was able to get up out of the uncomfortable position in which she had been lying, and in two or three minutes more she was once more three inches high.

She ran out of the house as quick as she could, and found quite a crowd of little animals waiting outside — guinea-pigs, white mice, squirrels, and "Bill" a little green lizard, that was being supported in the arms of one of the guinea-pigs, while another was giving it something out of a bottle. They all made a rush at her the moment she appeared, but Alice ran her hardest, and soon found herself in a thick wood.

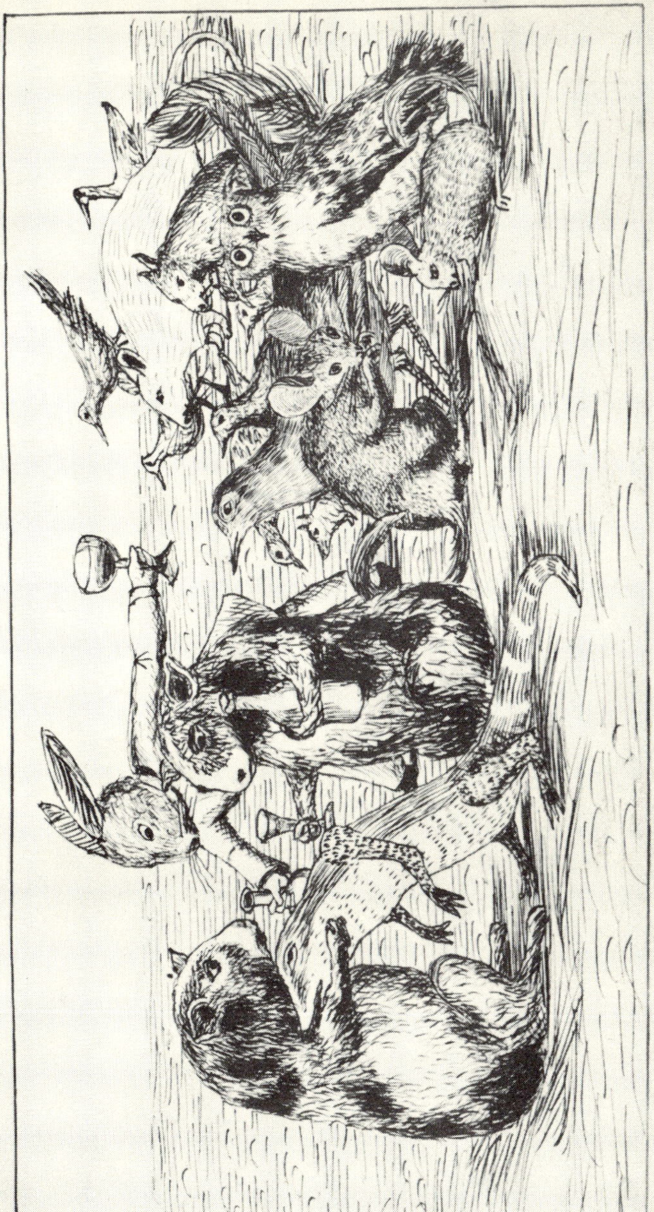

Chapter III

"The first thing I've got to do," said Alice to herself, as she wandered about in the wood, "is to grow to my right size, and the second thing is to find my way into that lovely garden. I think that will be the best plan."

It sounded an excellent plan, no doubt, and very neatly and simply arranged: the only difficulty was, that she had not the smallest idea how to set about it, and while she was peering anxiously among the trees round her, a little sharp bark just over her head made her look up in a great hurry.

An enormous puppy was looking down at her with large round eyes, and feebly stretching out one paw, trying to reach her: "poor thing!" said Alice in a coaxing tone, and she tried hard to whistle to it, but she was terribly alarmed all the while at the thought that it might be hungry, in which case it would probably devour her in spite of all her coaxing. Hardly knowing what she did, she picked up a little bit of stick, and held it out to the puppy: whereupon the puppy jumped into the air off all its feet at once, and with a yelp of delight rushed at the stick, and made believe to worry it: then Alice dodged behind a great thistle to keep herself from being run over, and, the moment she appeared at the other side, the puppy made another dart at the stick, and tumbled head over heels in its hurry to get hold: then Alice, thinking it was very like having a game of play with a cart-horse, and expecting every moment to be trampled under its feet, ran round the thistle again: then the puppy began a series of short charges at the stick, running a very little way forwards each time and a long way back, and barking hoarsely all the while, till at last it sat down a good way off, panting, with its tongue hanging out of its mouth, and its great eyes half shut.

This seemed to Alice a good opportunity for making her escape: she set off at once, and ran till the puppy's bark sounded quite faint in the distance, and till she was quite tired and out of breath.

"And yet what a dear little puppy it was!" said Alice, as she leant against a buttercup to rest herself, and fanned herself with her hat, "I should have liked teaching it tricks, if — if I'd only been the right size to do it! Oh! I'd nearly forgotten that I've got to grow up again! Let me see: how <u>is</u> it to be managed? I suppose I ought to eat or drink something or other, but the great question is, what?"

The great question certainly was, what? Alice looked all round her at the flowers and the blades of grass, but could not see anything that looked like the right thing to eat under the circumstances. There was a large mushroom near her, about the same height as herself, and when she had looked under it, and on both sides of it, and behind it, it occurred to her to look and see what was on the top of it.

She stretched herself up on tiptoe, and peeped over the edge of the mushroom,

and her eyes
immediately met
those of a large
blue caterpillar,
which was sitting
with its arms fold-
-ed, quietly smoking
a long hookah, and
taking not the least
notice of her or
of anything else.

For some
time they looked
at each other in
silence: at last
the caterpillar took the hookah out of its
mouth, and languidly addressed her.

"Who are you?" said the caterpillar.

This was not an encouraging opening
for a conversation: Alice replied rather shyly,
"I — I hardly know, sir, just at present —
at least I know who I *was* when I got
up this morning, but I think I must have
been changed several times since that."

"What do you mean by that?" said the
caterpillar, "explain yourself!"

"I can't explain *myself*, I'm afraid, sir,"

said Alice, "because I'm not myself, you see."

"I don't see", said the caterpillar.

"I'm afraid I ca'n't put it more clearly," Alice replied very politely, "for I ca'n't understand it myself, and really to be so many different sizes in one day is very confusing."

"It isn't," said the caterpillar.

"Well, perhaps you haven't found it so yet", said Alice, "but when you have to turn into a chrysalis, you know, and then after that into a butterfly, I should think it'll feel a little queer, don't you think so?"

"Not a bit," said the caterpillar.

"All I know is," said Alice, "it would feel queer to me."

"You!" said the caterpillar contemptuously, "who are you?"

Which brought them back again to the beginning of the conversation: Alice felt a little irritated at the caterpillar making such very short remarks, and she drew herself up and said very gravely "I think you ought to tell me who you are, first."

"Why?" said the caterpillar.

Here was another puzzling question:

and as Alice had no reason ready, and the caterpillar seemed to be in a very bad temper, she turned round and walked away.

"Come back!" the caterpillar called after her, "I've something important to say!"

This sounded promising: Alice turned and came back again.

"Keep your temper," said the caterpillar.

"Is that all?" said Alice, swallowing down her anger as well as she could.

"No," said the caterpillar.

Alice thought she might as well wait, as she had nothing else to do, and perhaps after all the caterpillar might tell her something worth hearing. For some minutes it puffed away at its hookah without speaking, but at last it unfolded its arms, took the hookah out of its mouth again, and said "So you think you're changed, do you?"

"Yes, sir," said Alice, "I can't remember the things I used to know — I've tried to say "How doth the little busy bee" and it came all different!"

"Try and repeat "You are old, father William"," said the caterpillar.

Alice folded her hands, and began:

52.

1.

"You are old, father William," the young man said,
"And your hair is exceedingly white:
And yet you incessantly stand on your head—
Do you think, at your age, it is right?"

2.

"In my youth," father William replied to his son,
"I feared it might injure the brain:
But now that I'm perfectly sure I have none,
Why, I do it again and again."

54

3.

"You are old," said the youth, "as I mentioned before,
    And have grown most uncommonly fat:
Yet you turned a back-somersault in at the door—
    Pray what is the reason of that?"

4.

"In my youth," said the sage, as he shook his gray locks,
    "I kept all my limbs very supple
By the use of this ointment, five shillings the box—
    Allow me to sell you a couple."

56.

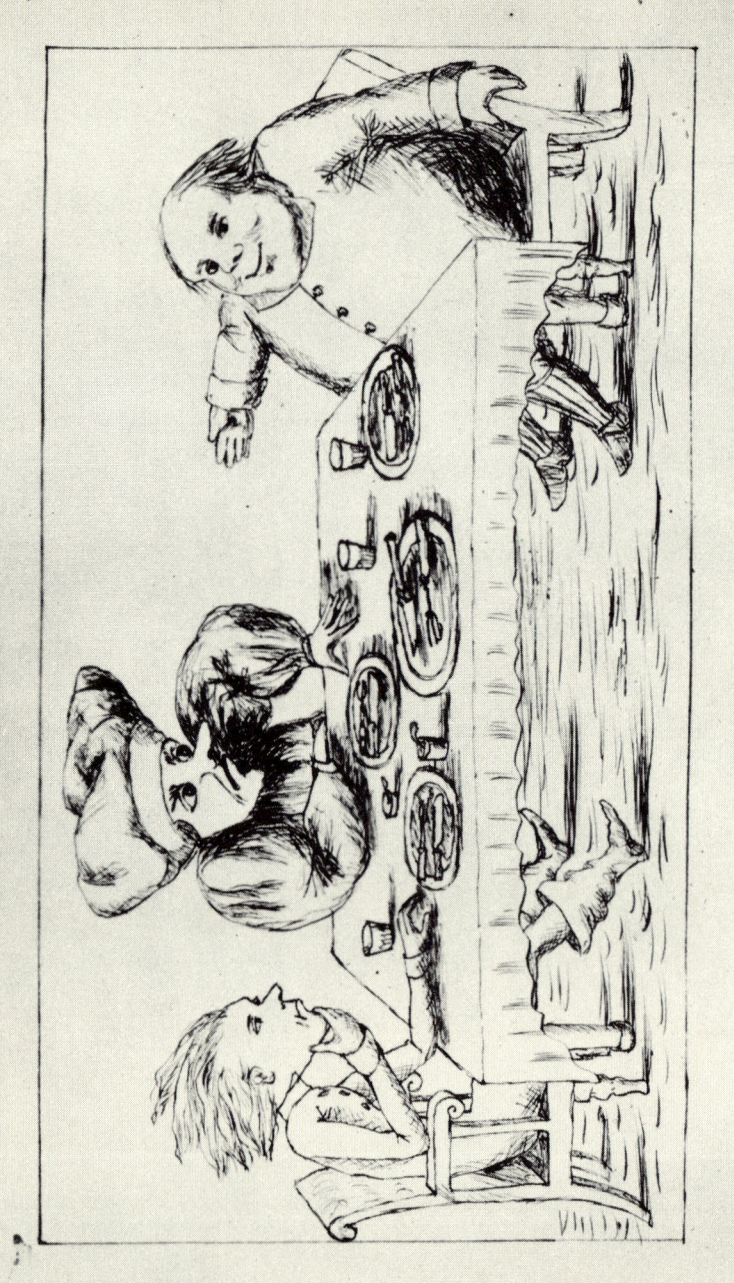

5.

"You are old," said the youth, "and your jaws are too weak
"For anything tougher than suet:
Yet you eat all the goose, with the bones and the beak —
Pray, how did you manage to do it?"

6.

"In my youth," said the old man, "I took to the law,
And argued each case with my wife,
And the muscular strength, which it gave to my jaw,
Has lasted the rest of my life."

58.

7.

"You are old", said the youth, "one would hardly suppose
"That your eye was as steady as ever:
Yet you balanced an eel on the end of your nose —
What made you so <u>awfully</u> clever?"

8.

"I have answered three questions, and that is enough,"
Said his father, "don't give yourself airs!
"Do you think I can listen all day to such stuff?
Be off, or I'll kick you down stairs!"

"That is not said right," said the caterpillar.

"Not quite right, I'm afraid," said Alice timidly, "some of the words have got altered."

"It is wrong from beginning to end," said the caterpillar decidedly, and there was silence for some minutes: the caterpillar was the first to speak.

"What size do you want to be?" it asked.

"Oh, I'm not particular as to size," Alice hastily replied, "only one doesn't like changing so often, you know."

"Are you content now?" said the caterpillar.

"Well, I should like to be a little larger, sir, if you wouldn't mind," said Alice, "three inches is such a wretched height to be."

"It is a very good height indeed!" said the caterpillar loudly and angrily, rearing itself straight up as it spoke (it was exactly three inches high).

"But I'm not used to it!" pleaded poor Alice in a piteous tone, and she thought to herself "I wish the creatures wouldn't be so easily offended!"

"You'll get used to it in time", said the caterpillar, and it put the hookah into its mouth, and began smoking again.

This time Alice waited quietly until it chose to speak again: in a few minutes the caterpillar took the hookah out of its mouth, and got down off the mushroom, and crawled away into the grass, merely remarking as it went: "the top will make you grow taller, and the stalk will make you grow shorter."

"The top of <u>what</u>? the stalk of <u>what</u>?" thought Alice.

"Of the mushroom," said the caterpillar, just as if she had asked it aloud, and in another moment it was out of sight.

Alice remained looking thoughtfully at the mushroom for a minute, and then picked it and carefully broke it in two, taking the stalk in one hand, and the top in the other. "<u>Which</u> does the stalk do?" she said, and nibbled a little bit of it to try: the next moment she felt a violent blow on her chin: it had struck her foot!

She was a good deal frightened by this very sudden change, but as she did not shrink any further, and had not dropped the top of the mushroom, she did not give up hope yet. There was hardly room to open her mouth, with her chin pressing against her foot, but she did it at last, and managed to bite off a little bit of the top of the mushroom.

* * * * *

"Come! my head's free at last!" said Alice in a tone of delight, which changed into alarm in another moment, when she found that her shoulders were nowhere to be seen: she looked down upon an immense length of neck, which seemed to rise like a stalk out of a sea of green leaves that lay far below her.

"What *can* all that green stuff be?" said Alice, "and where *have* my shoulders got to? And oh! my poor hands! how is it I can't see you?" She was moving them about as she spoke, but no result seemed to follow, except a little rustling among the leaves. Then she tried to bring her head down to her hands, and was delighted to find that her neck would bend about easily in every direction, like a serpent. She had just succeeded in bending it down in a beautiful zig-zag, and was going to dive in among the leaves, which she found to be the tops of the trees of the wood she had been wandering in, when a sharp hiss made her draw back: a large pigeon had flown into her face, and was violently beating her with its wings.

"Serpent!" screamed the pigeon.

"I'm *not* a serpent!" said Alice indignantly, "let me alone!"

"I've tried every way!" the pigeon said desperately, with a kind of sob: "nothing seems to suit 'em!"

"I haven't the least idea what you mean," said Alice.

"I've tried the roots of trees, and I've tried banks, and I've tried hedges," the pigeon went on without attending to her, "but them serpents! There's no pleasing 'em!"

Alice was more and more puzzled, but she thought there was no use in saying anything till the pigeon had finished.

"As if it wasn't trouble enough hatching the eggs!" said the pigeon, "without being on the look out for serpents, day and night! Why, I haven't had a wink of sleep these three weeks!"

"I'm very sorry you've been annoyed," said Alice, beginning to see its meaning.

"And just as I'd taken the highest tree in the wood," said the pigeon raising its voice to a shriek, "and was just thinking I was free of 'em at last, they must needs come down from the sky! Ugh! Serpent!"

"But I'm _not_ a serpent," said Alice, "I'm a — I'm a —"

"Well! What are you?" said the pigeon, "I see you're trying to invent something."

"I— I'm a little girl," said Alice, rather doubtfully, as she remembered the number of changes she had gone through.

"A likely story indeed!" said the pigeon, "I've seen a good many of them in my time, but never *one* with such a neck as yours! No, you're a serpent, I know *that* well enough! I suppose you'll tell me next that you never tasted an egg!"

"I *have* tasted eggs, certainly," said Alice, who was a very truthful child, "but indeed I don't want any of yours. I don't like them raw."

"Well, be off, then!" said the pigeon, and settled down into its nest again. Alice crouched down among the trees, as well as she could, as her neck kept getting entangled among the branches, and several times she had to stop and untwist it. Soon she remembered the pieces of mushroom which she still held in her hands, and set to work very carefully, nibbling first at one and then at the other, and growing sometimes taller and sometimes shorter, until she had succeeded in bringing herself down to her usual size.

It was so long since she had been of the right size that it felt quite strange at first, but she got quite used to it in a minute or two, and began talking to herself as usual: "well! there's half my plan done now! How puzzling all these changes are! I'm never sure what I'm going to be, from one minute to another! However, I've got to my right size again: the next thing is, to get into that beautiful garden — how _is_ that to be done, I wonder?"

Just as she said this, she noticed that one of the trees had a doorway leading right into it. "That's very curious!" she thought, "but everything's curious today: I may as well go in." And in she went.

Once more she found herself in the long hall, and close to the little glass table: "now, I'll manage better this time" she said to herself, and began by taking the little golden key, and unlocking the door that led into the garden. Then she set to work eating the pieces of mushroom till she was about fifteen inches high: then she walked down the little passage: and then — she found herself at last in the beautiful garden, among the bright flowerbeds and the cool fountains.

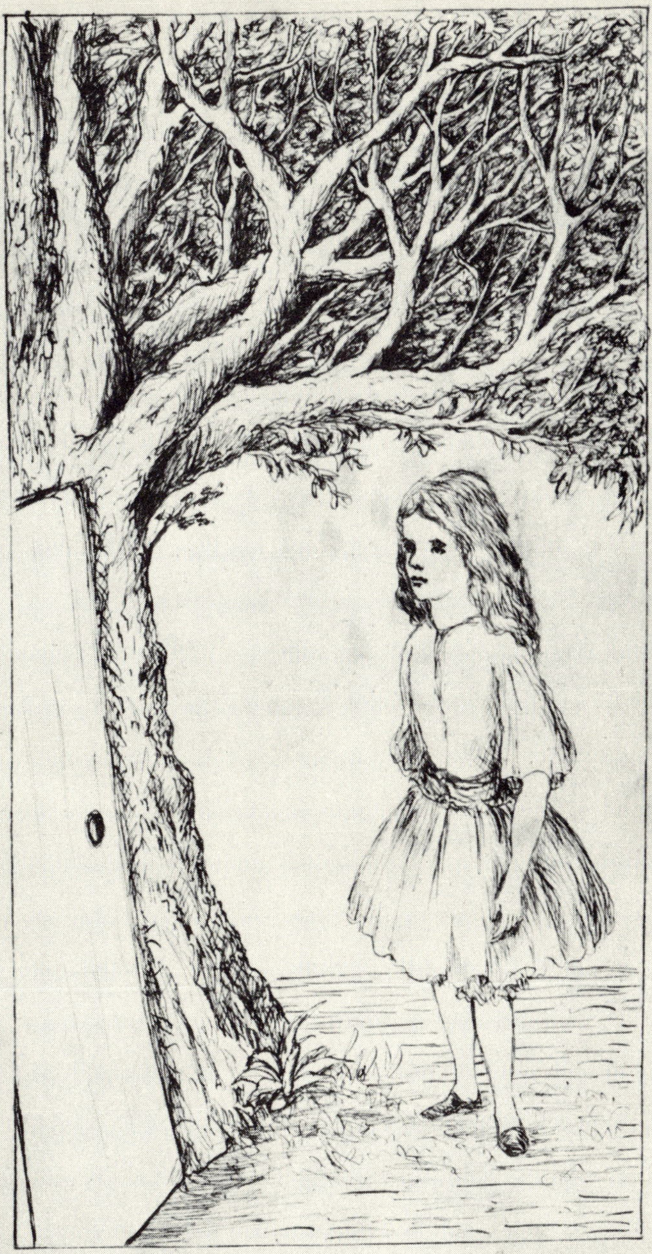

Chapter IV

A large rose tree stood near the entrance of the garden: the roses on it were white, but there were three gardeners at it, busily painting them red. This Alice thought a very curious thing, and she went near to watch them, and just as she came up she heard one of them say "look out, Five! Don't go splashing paint over me like that!"

"I couldn't help it," said Five in a sulky tone, "Seven jogged my elbow."

On which Seven lifted up his head and said "that's right, Five! Always lay the blame on others!"

"You'd better not talk!" said Five, "I

heard the Queen say only yesterday she thought of having you beheaded!"

"What for?" said the one who had spoken first.

"That's not your business, Two!" said Seven.

"Yes, it *is* his business!" said Five, "and I'll tell him: it was for bringing tulip-roots to the cook instead of potatoes."

Seven flung down his brush, and had just begun "well! Of all the unjust things——" when his eye fell upon Alice, and he stopped suddenly: the others looked round, and all of them took off their hats and bowed low.

"Would you tell me, please," said Alice timidly, "why you are painting those roses?"

Five and Seven looked at Two, but said nothing: Two began, in a low voice, "why, Miss, the fact is, this ought to have been a red rose tree, and we put a white one in by mistake, and if the Queen was to find it out, we should all have our heads cut off. So, you see, we're doing our best, before she comes, to——" At this moment Five, who had been looking anxiously across the garden called out "the Queen! the Queen!" and the three gardeners instantly threw themselves flat upon their faces. There was a sound of many footsteps, and Alice looked round, eager to see the Queen.

First came ten soldiers carrying clubs: these were all shaped like the three gardeners, flat and oblong, with their hands and feet at the corners: next the ten courtiers; these were all ornamented with diamonds, and walked two and two, as the soldiers did. After these came the Royal children: there were ten of them, and the little dears came jumping merrily along, hand in hand, in couples: they were all ornamented with hearts. Next came the guests, mostly kings and queens, among whom Alice recognised the white rabbit: it was talking in a hurried nervous manner, smiling at everything that was said, and went by without noticing her. Then followed the Knave of Hearts, carrying the King's crown on a cushion, and, last of all this grand procession, came THE KING AND QUEEN OF HEARTS.

When the procession came opposite to Alice, they all stopped and looked at her, and

37 71

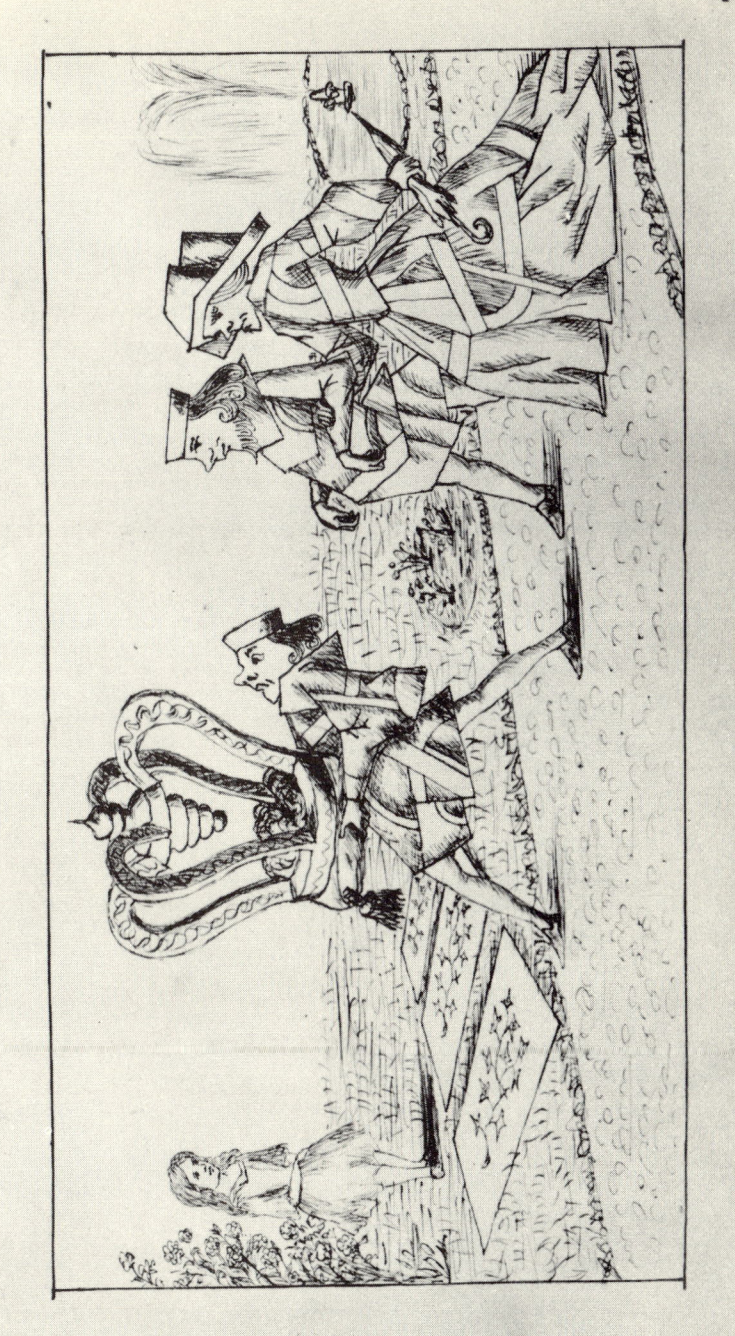

the Queen said severely "who is this?" She said it to the Knave of Hearts, who only bowed and smiled in reply.

"Idiot!" said the Queen, turning up her nose, and asked Alice "what's your name?"

"My name is Alice, so please your Majesty," said Alice boldly, for she thought to herself "why, they're only a pack of cards! I needn't be afraid of them!"

"Who are these?" said the Queen, pointing to the three gardeners lying round the rose tree, for, as they were lying on their faces, and the pattern on their backs was the same as the rest of the pack, she could not tell whether they were gardeners, or soldiers, or courtiers, or three of her own children.

"How should _I_ know?" said Alice, surprised at her own courage, "it's no business of _mine_."

The Queen turned crimson with fury, and, after glaring at her for a minute, began in a voice of thunder "off with her——"

"Nonsense!" said Alice, very loudly and decidedly, and the Queen was silent.

The King laid his hand upon her arm, and said timidly "remember, my dear! She is only a child!"

The Queen turned angrily away from him, and said to the Knave "turn them over!"

The Knave did so, very carefully, with one foot.

"Get up!" said the Queen, in a shrill loud voice, and the three gardeners instantly jumped up, and began bowing to the King, the Queen, the Royal children, and everybody else.

"Leave off that!" screamed the Queen, "you make me giddy." And then, turning to the rose tree, she went on "what _have_ you been doing here?"

"May it please your Majesty", said Two very humbly, going down on one knee as he spoke, "we were trying——"

"_I_ see!" said the Queen, who had meantime been examining the roses, "off with their heads!" and the procession moved on, three of the soldiers remaining behind to execute the three unfortunate gardeners, who ran to Alice for protection.

"You shan't be beheaded!" said Alice, and she put them into her pocket: the three soldiers marched once round her, looking for them, and then quietly marched off after the others.

"Are their heads off?" shouted the Queen.

"Their heads are gone," the soldiers shouted in reply, "if it please your Majesty!"

"That's right!" shouted the Queen, "can you play croquet?"

The soldiers were silent, and looked at Alice, as the question was evidently meant for her.

"Yes!" shouted Alice at the top of her voice.

"Come on then!" roared the Queen, and Alice joined the procession, wondering very much what would happen next.

"It's — its a very fine day!" said a timid little voice: she was walking by the white rabbit, who was peeping anxiously into her face.

"Very," said Alice, "where's the Marchioness?"

"Hush, hush!" said the rabbit in a low voice, "she'll hear you. The Queen's the Marchioness: didn't you know that?"

"No, I didn't," said Alice, "what of?"

"Queen of Hearts," said the rabbit in a whisper, putting its mouth close to her ear, "and Marchioness of Mock Turtles."

"What are they?" said Alice, but there was no time for the answer, for they had reached the croquet-ground, and the game began instantly.

Alice thought she had never seen such a curious croquet-ground in all her life: it was all in ridges and furrows: the croquet-balls were live hedgehogs, the mallets live ostriches, and the soldiers had to double themselves up, and stand

39 75

on their feet and hands, to make the arches.

The chief difficulty which Alice found at first was to manage her ostrich: she got its body tucked away, comfortably enough, under her arm, with its legs hanging down, but generally, just as she had got its neck straightened out nicely, and was going to give a blow with its head, it would twist itself round, and look up into her face, with such a puzzled expression that she could not help bursting out laughing: and when she had got its head down, and was going to begin again, it was very confusing to find that the hedgehog had unrolled itself, and was in the act of crawling away: besides all this, there was generally a ridge or a furrow in her way, wherever she wanted to send the hedgehog to, and as the doubled-up soldiers were always getting up and walking off to other parts of the ground, Alice soon came to the conclusion that it was a very difficult game indeed.

The players all played at once without waiting for turns, and quarrelled all the while at the tops of their voices, and in a very few minutes the Queen was in a furious passion, and went stamping about and shouting "off with his head!" or "off with her head!" about once in a minute. All those whom she sentenced were taken into custody by the soldiers, who of course had to leave off being arches to do this, so that, by the end of half an hour or so, there were no arches left, and all the players, except the King, the Queen, and Alice, were in custody, and under sentence of execution.

Then the Queen left off, quite out of breath, and said to Alice "have you seen the Mock Turtle?"

"No," said Alice, "I don't even know what a Mock Turtle is."

"Come on then," said the Queen, "and it shall tell you its history."

As they walked off together, Alice heard the King say in a low voice, to the company generally, "you are all pardoned."

"Come, that's a good thing!" thought Alice, who had felt quite grieved at the number of executions which the Queen had ordered.

They very soon came upon a Gryphon, which lay fast asleep in the sun: (if you don't know what a Gryphon is, look at the picture): "up, lazy thing!" said the Queen, "and take this young lady to see the Mock Turtle, and to hear its history. I must go back and see after some executions I ordered," and she walked off, leaving Alice with the Gryphon. Alice did not quite like the look of the creature, but on the whole she thought it quite as safe to stay as to go after that savage Queen: so she waited.

The Gryphon sat up and rubbed its eyes: then it watched the Queen till she was out of sight: then it chuckled. "What fun!" said the Gryphon, half to itself, half to Alice.

"What *is* the fun?" said Alice.

"Why, *she*," said the Gryphon; "it's all her fancy, that: they never executes nobody, you know: come on!"

"Everybody says 'come on!' here," thought Alice, as she walked slowly after the Gryphon; "I never was ordered about so before in all my life — never!"

They had not gone far before they saw the Mock Turtle in the distance, sitting sad and lonely on a little ledge of rock, and, as they came nearer, Alice could hear it sighing as if it its heart would break. She pitied it deeply: "what is its sorrow?" she asked the Gryphon, and the Gryphon answered, very nearly in the same words as before, "it's all its fancy, that: it hasn't got no sorrow, you know: come on!"

So they went up to the Mock Turtle, who looked at them with large eyes full of tears, but said nothing.

"This here young lady" said the Gryphon,

"wants for to know your history, she do."

"I'll tell it," said the Mock Turtle, in a deep hollow tone, "sit down, and don't speak till I've finished."

So they sat down, and no one spoke for some minutes: Alice thought to herself "I don't see how it can *ever* finish, if it doesn't begin," but she waited patiently.

"Once," said the Mock Turtle at last, with a deep sigh, "I was a real Turtle."

These words were followed by a very long silence, broken only by an occasional ex--clamation of "hjckrrh!" from the Gryphon, and the constant heavy sobbing of the Mock Turtle. Alice was very nearly getting up and saying, "thank you, sir, for your interesting story," but she could not help thinking there *must* be more to come, so she sat still and said nothing.

"When we were little," the Mock Turtle went on, more calmly, though still sobbing a little now and then, "we went to school in the sea. The master was an old Turtle—we used to call him Tortoise—"

"Why did you call him Tortoise, if he wasn't one?" asked Alice.

"We called him Tortoise because he taught us," said the Mock Turtle angrily, "really you are very dull!"

"You ought to be ashamed of yourself for asking such a simple question," added the Gryphon, and then they both sat silent and looked at poor Alice, who felt ready to sink into the earth: at last the Gryphon said to the Mock Turtle, "get on, old fellow! Don't be all day!" and the Mock Turtle went on in these words:

"You may not have lived much under the sea—" ("I haven't," said Alice,) "and perhaps you were never even introduced to a lobster—" (Alice began to say "I once tasted—" but hastily checked herself, and said "no, never," instead,) "so you can have no idea what a delightful thing a Lobster Quadrille is!"

"No, indeed," said Alice, "what sort of a thing is it?"

"Why," said the Gryphon, "you form into a line along the sea shore—"

"Two lines!" cried the Mock Turtle, "seals, turtles, salmon, and so on—advance twice—"

"Each with a lobster as partner!" cried the Gryphon.

82

"Of course", the Mock Turtle said, "advance twice, set to partners —"

"Change lobsters, and retire in same order —" interrupted the Gryphon.

"Then, you know," continued the Mock Turtle, "you throw the —"

"The lobsters!" shouted the Gryphon, with a bound into the air.

"As far out to sea as you can —"

"Swim after them!" screamed the Gryphon.

"Turn a somersault in the sea!" cried the Mock Turtle, capering wildly about.

"Change lobsters again!" yelled the Gryphon at the top of its voice, "and then —"

"That's all," said the Mock Turtle, suddenly dropping its voice, and the two creatures, who had been jumping about like mad things all this time, sat down again very sadly and quietly, and looked at Alice.

"It must be a very pretty dance," said Alice timidly.

"Would you like to see a little of it?" said the Mock Turtle.

"Very much indeed," said Alice.

"Come, let's try the first figure!" said the Mock Turtle to the Gryphon, "we can do it without lobsters, you know. Which shall sing?"

"Oh! you sing!" said the Gryphon, "I've forgotten the words."

So they began solemnly dancing 'round and round Alice, every now and then treading on her toes when they came too close, and waving their fore-paws to mark the time, while the Mock Turtle sang, slowly and sadly, these words:

"Beneath the waters of the sea
Are lobsters thick as thick can be—
They love to dance with you and me,
My own, my gentle Salmon!"

The Gryphon joined in singing the chorus, which was:

"Salmon come up! Salmon go down!
Salmon come twist your tail around!
Of all the fishes of the sea
There's none so good as Salmon!"

"Thank you", said Alice, feeling very glad that the figure was over.

"Shall we try the second figure?" said the Gryphon, "or would you prefer a song?"

"Oh, a song, please!" Alice replied, so eagerly, that the Gryphon said, in a rather offended tone, "hm! no accounting for tastes! Sing her 'Mock Turtle Soup', will you, old fellow!"

The Mock Turtle sighed deeply, and began, in a voice sometimes choked with sobs, to sing this:

"Beautiful Soup, so rich and green,
Waiting in a hot tureen!
Who for such dainties would not stoop?
Soup of the evening, beautiful Soup!
Soup of the evening, beautiful Soup!
 Beau—ootiful Soo—oop!
 Beau—ootiful Soo—oop!
Soo—oop of the e—e—evening,
 Beautiful beautiful Soup!

"Chorus again!" cried the Gryphon, and

the Mock Turtle had just begun to repeat it, when a cry of "the trial's beginning!" was heard in the distance.

"Come on!" cried the Gryphon, and, taking Alice by the hand, he hurried off, without waiting for the end of the song.

"What trial is it?" panted Alice as she ran, but the Gryphon only answered "come on!" and ran the faster, and more and more faintly came, borne on the breeze that followed them, the melancholy words:

"Soo—oop of the e-e-evening,
Beautiful beautiful Soup!"

The King and Queen were seated on their throne when they arrived, with a great crowd assembled around them: the Knave was in custody: and before the King stood the white rabbit, with a trumpet in one hand, and a scroll of parchment in the other.

"Herald! read the accusation!" said the King.

On this the white rabbit blew three blasts on the trumpet, and then unrolled the parchment scroll, and read as follows:

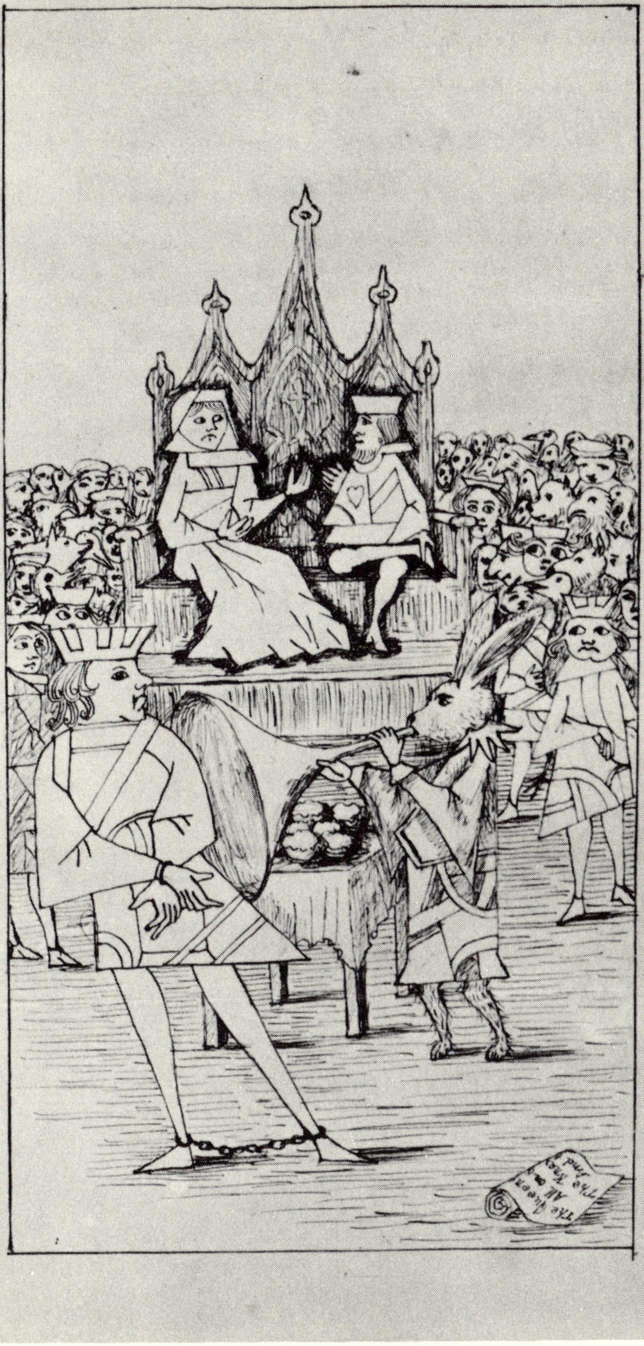

"The Queen of Hearts she made some tarts
   All on a summer day:
The Knave of Hearts he stole those tarts,
   And took them quite away!"

"Now for the evidence," said the King, "and then the sentence."

"No!" said the Queen, "first the sentence, and then the evidence!"

"Nonsense!" cried Alice, so loudly that everybody jumped, "the idea of having the sentence first!"

"Hold your tongue!" said the Queen.

"I won't!" said Alice, "you're nothing but a pack of cards! Who cares for you?"

At this the whole pack rose up into the air, and came flying down upon her: she gave a little scream of fright, and tried to beat them off, and found herself lying on the bank, with her head in the lap of her sister, who was gently brushing away some leaves that had fluttered down from the trees on to her face.

"Wake up! Alice dear!" said her sister, "what a nice long sleep you've had!"

"Oh, I've had such a curious dream!" said Alice, and she told her sister all her Adventures Under Ground, as you have read them, and when she had finished, her sister kissed her and said "it _was_ a curious dream, dear, certainly! But now run in to your tea: it's getting late."

So Alice ran off, thinking while she ran (as well she might) what a wonderful dream it had been.

But her sister sat there some while longer, watching the setting sun, and thinking of little Alice and her Adventures, till she too began dreaming after a fashion, and this was her dream:

She saw an ancient city, and a quiet river winding near it along the plain, and up the stream went slowly gliding a boat with a merry party of children on board — she could hear their voices and laughter like music over the water — and among them was another little Alice, who sat listening with bright eager eyes to a tale that was being told, and she listened for the words of the tale, and lo! it was the dream of her own little sister. So the boat wound slowly along, beneath the bright summer-day, with its merry crew and its music of voices and laughter, till it passed round one of the many turnings of the stream, and she saw it no more.

Then she thought, (in a dream within the dream, as it were,) how this same little Alice would, in the after-time, be herself a grown woman: and how she would keep, through her riper years, the simple and loving heart of her childhood: and how she would gather around her other little children, and make _their_ eyes bright and eager with many a wonderful tale, perhaps even with these very adventures of the little Alice of long-ago: and how she would feel with all their simple sorrows, and find a pleasure in all their simple joys, remembering her own child-life, and the happy summer days.

happy summer days.

THE END.

ALICE'S ADVENTURES
UNDER GROUND

*BEING A FACSIMILE OF THE
ORIGINAL MS. BOOK
AFTERWARDS DEVELOPED INTO
"ALICE'S ADVENTURES IN WONDERLAND"*

BY

LEWIS CARROLL

*WITH THIRTY-SEVEN ILLUSTRATIONS
BY THE AUTHOR*

PRICE FOUR SHILLINGS

London
MACMILLAN AND CO.
AND NEW YORK
1886

[*The Right of Translation and Reproduction is Reserved.*]

RICHARD CLAY AND SONS,
LONDON AND BUNGAY.

" *Who will Riddle me the How and the Why?* "

So questions one of England's sweetest singers. The "How?" has already been told, after a fashion, in the verses prefixed to " Alice in Wonderland"; and some other memories of that happy summer day are set down, for those who care to see them, in this little book——the germ that was to grow into the published volume. But the " Why?" cannot, and need not, be put into words. Those for whom a child's mind is a sealed book, and who see no divinity in a child's smile, would read such words in vain: while for any one that has ever loved one true child, no words are needed. For he will have known the awe that falls on one in the presence of a spirit fresh from GOD'S *hands, on whom no shadow of sin, and but the outermost fringe of the shadow of sorrow, has yet fallen: he will have felt the bitter contrast between the haunting selfishness that spoils his best deeds and the life that is but an overflowing love——for I think a child's* first *attitude to the world is a simple love for all living things: and he will have learned that the best work a man can do is when he works for love's sake only, with no thought of name, or gain, or earthly reward. No deed of ours, I suppose, on this side the grave, is really unselfish: yet if one can put forth all one's powers in a task where nothing of reward is* hoped for but a little child's whispered thanks, and the airy touch of a little child's pure lips, one seems to come somewhere near to this.

There was no idea of publication in my mind when I wrote this little book: that was wholly an afterthought, pressed on me by the "*perhaps too partial friends*" who always have to bear the blame when a writer rushes into print: and I can truly say that no praise of theirs has ever given me one hundredth part of the pleasure it has been to think of the sick children in hospitals (where it has been a delight to me to send copies) forgetting, for a few bright hours, their pain and weariness——perhaps thinking lovingly of the unknown writer of the tale——perhaps even putting up a childish prayer (and oh, how much it needs!) for one who can but dimly hope to stand, some day, not quite out of sight of those pure young faces, before the great white throne. "I am very sure," writes a lady-visitor at a Home for Sick Children, "that there will be many loving earnest prayers for you on Easter morning from the children."

I would like to quote further from her letters, as embodying a *suggestion* that may perhaps thus come to the notice of some one able and willing to carry it out.

"I want you to send me one of your Easter Greetings for a very dear child who is dying at our Home. She is just fading away, and 'Alice' has brightened some of the weary hours in her illness, and I know that letter would be such a delight to her——especially if you would put 'Minnie' at the top, and she could know you had sent it for her. She *knows* you, and would so value it. . . She suffers so much that I long for what I know would so please her."

. . . . . . "Thank you very much for sending me the letter, and for writing Minnie's name. .... *I am quite sure that all these children will say a loving prayer for the 'Alice-man' on Easter Day: and I am sure the letter will help the little ones to the real Easter joy. How I do wish that you, who have won the hearts and confidence of so many children, would do for them what is so very near my heart, and yet what no one will do, viz. write a book for children about* GOD *and themselves, which is not goody, and which begins at the right end, about religion, to make them see what it really is. I get quite miserable very often over the children I come across: hardly any of them have an idea of* really *knowing that* GOD *loves them, or of loving and confiding in Him. They will love and trust* me, *and be sure that* I *want them to be happy, and will not let them suffer more than is necessary: but as for going to Him in the same way, they would never think of it. They are dreadfully afraid of Him, if they think of Him at all, which they generally only do when they have been naughty, and they look on all connected with Him as very grave and dull: and, when they are full of fun and thoroughly happy, I am sure they unconsciously hope He is not looking. I am sure I don't wonder they think of Him in this way, for people* never *talk of Him in connection with what makes their little lives the brightest. If they are naughty, people put on solemn faces, and say He is very angry or shocked, or something which frightens them: and, for the rest, He is talked about only in a way that makes them think of church and having to be quiet. As for being taught that all Joy and all Gladness and Brightness is His Joy—that He is wearying for them to be happy, and is not hard and stern, but always doing things to make their days brighter, and caring for them so tenderly, and wanting them to run to Him with* all *their little joys and sorrows, they are not taught that. I do so long to make them trust Him as they trust us, to feel that He will 'take their part' as they do with us in their little woes, and to go to Him in their plays and enjoyments and not only when they say their prayers. I was quite grateful to one little dot, a short time ago, who said to his mother 'when I am in bed, I put out my hand to see if I can feel* JESUS *and my angel. I thought perhaps* in the dark *they'd touch me, but they never have yet.' I do so want them to* want *to go to Him, and to feel how, if He is there, it* must *be happy."*

Let me add—for I feel I have drifted into far too serious a vein for a preface to a fairy-tale—the deliciously naïve remark of a very dear child-friend, whom I asked, after an acquaintance of two or three days, if she had read 'Alice' and the 'Looking-Glass.' "Oh yes," she replied readily, " I've read both of them! And I think" (this more slowly and thoughtfully) " I think ' Through the Looking-Glass' is more *stupid than 'Alice's Adventures.' Don't you think so ? " But this was a question I felt it would be hardly discreet for me to enter upon.*

LEWIS CARROLL.

Dec. 1886.

POSTSCRIPT.

The profits, if any, of this book will be given to Children's Hospitals and Convalescent Homes for Sick Children: and the accounts, down to June 30 in each year, will be published in the St. James's Gazette, on the second Tuesday of the following December.

P.P.S.—The thought, so prettily expressed by the little boy, is also to be found in Longfellow's "Hiawatha," where he appeals to those who believe

"*That the feeble hands and helpless,
Groping blindly in the darkness,
Touch* GOD'S *right hand in that darkness,
And are lifted up and strengthened.*"

CONTENTS.

CHAPTER		PAGE
I.	DOWN THE RABBIT-HOLE. THE POOL OF TEARS . . .	1
II.	A LONG TALE. THE RABBIT SENDS IN A LITTLE BILL .	24
III.	ADVICE FROM A CATERPILLAR	46
IV.	THE QUEEN'S CROQUET-GROUND. THE MOCK TURTLE'S STORY. THE LOBSTER QUADRILLE. WHO STOLE THE TARTS ?	68

AN EASTER GREETING

TO

EVERY CHILD WHO LOVES

"𝔄𝔩𝔦𝔠𝔢."

DEAR CHILD,

 Please to fancy, if you can, that you are reading a real letter, from a real friend whom you have seen, and whose voice you can seem to yourself to hear wishing you, as I do now with all my heart, a happy Easter.

 Do you know that delicious dreamy feeling when one first wakes on a summer morning, with the twitter of birds in the air, and the fresh breeze coming in at the open window——when, lying lazily with eyes half shut, one sees as in a dream green boughs waving, or waters rippling in a golden light? It is a pleasure very near to sadness, bringing tears to one's eyes like a beautiful picture or poem. And is not that a Mother's gentle hand that undraws your curtains, and a Mother's sweet voice that summons you to rise? To rise and forget, in the bright sunlight, the ugly dreams that frightened you so when all was dark——to rise and enjoy another happy day, first kneeling to thank that unseen Friend, who sends you the beautiful sun?

Are these strange words from a writer of such tales as "Alice"? And is this a strange letter to find in a book of nonsense? It may be so. Some perhaps may blame me for thus mixing together things grave and gay; others may smile and think it odd that any one should speak of solemn things at all, except in church and on a Sunday: but I think——nay, I am sure——that some children will read this gently and lovingly, and in the spirit in which I have written it.

For I do not believe God means us thus to divide life into two halves——to wear a grave face on Sunday, and to think it out-of-place to even so much as mention Him on a week-day. Do you think He cares to see only kneeling figures, and to hear only tones of prayer——and that He does not also love to see the lambs leaping in the sunlight, and to hear the merry voices of the children, as they roll among the hay? Surely their innocent laughter is as sweet in His ears as the grandest anthem that ever rolled up from the " dim religious light" of some solemn cathedral?

And if I have written anything to add to those stores of innocent and healthy amusement that are laid up in books for the children I love so well, it is surely something I may hope to look back upon without shame and sorrow (as how much of life must then be recalled!) when my *turn comes to walk through the valley of shadows.*

This Easter sun will rise on you, dear child, feeling your " life in every limb," and eager to rush out into the fresh morning air

An Easter Greeting.

——*and many an Easter-day will come and go, before it finds you feeble and gray-headed, creeping wearily out to bask once more in the sunlight——but it is good, even now, to think sometimes of that great morning when the " Sun of Righteousness shall arise with healing in his wings."*

Surely your gladness need not be the less for the thought that you will one day see a brighter dawn than this——when lovelier sights will meet your eyes than any waving trees or rippling waters—— when angel-hands shall undraw your curtains, and sweeter tones than ever loving Mother breathed shall wake you to a new and glorious day——and when all the sadness, and the sin, that darkened life on this little earth, shall be forgotten like the dreams of a night that is past!

Your affectionate friend,

LEWIS CARROLL.

Easter, 1876.

CHRISTMAS GREETINGS.

[FROM A FAIRY TO A CHILD.]

LADY dear, if Fairies may
For a moment lay aside
Cunning tricks and elfish play,
'Tis at happy Christmas-tide.

We have heard the children say—
Gentle children, whom we love—
Long ago, on Christmas Day,
Came a message from above.

Still, as Christmas-tide comes round,
They remember it again—
Echo still the joyful sound
"Peace on earth, good-will to men!"

Yet the hearts must childlike be
Where such heavenly guests abide;
Unto children, in their glee,
All the year is Christmas-tide!

Thus, forgetting tricks and play
For a moment, Lady dear,
We would wish you, if we may,
Merry Christmas, glad New Year!

LEWIS CARROLL.

Christmas, 1867.

RICHARD CLAY AND SONS, LONDON AND BUNGAY.

WORKS BY LEWIS CARROLL.

PUBLISHED BY

MACMILLAN AND CO., LONDON.

ALICE'S ADVENTURES IN WONDERLAND.
With Forty-two Illustrations by TENNIEL. (First published in 1865.) Crown 8vo, cloth, gilt edges, price 6s. Seventy-eighth Thousand.

AVENTURES D'ALICE AU PAYS DES MERVEILLES. Traduit de l'Anglais par Henri Bué. Ouvrage illustré de 42 Vignettes par JOHN TENNIEL. (First published in 1869.) Crown 8vo, cloth, gilt edges, price 6s.

Alice's Abenteuer im Wunderland. Aus dem Englischen, von Antonie Zimmermann. Mit 42 Illustrationen von John Tenniel. (First published in 1869.) Crown 8vo, cloth, gilt edges, price 6s.

LE AVVENTURE D'ALICE NEL PAESE DELLE MERAVIGLIE. Tradotte dall' Inglese da T. PIETROCÒLA-ROSSETTI. Con 42 Vignette di GIOVANNI TENNIEL. (First published in 1872.) Crown 8vo, cloth, gilt edges, price 6s.

THROUGH THE LOOKING-GLASS AND WHAT ALICE FOUND THERE. With Fifty Illustrations by TENNIEL. (First published in 1871.) Crown 8vo, cloth, gilt edges, price 6s. Fifty sixth Thousand.

RHYME? AND REASON? With Sixty-five Illustrations by ARTHUR B. FROST, and Nine by HENRY HOLIDAY. (This book, first published in 1883, is a reprint, with a few additions, of the comic portion of "Phantasmagoria and other Poems," published in 1869, and of "The Hunting of the Snark," published in 1876. Mr. Frost's pictures are new.) Crown 8vo, cloth, coloured edges, price 6s. Fifth Thousand.

WORKS BY LEWIS CARROLL.

PUBLISHED BY

MACMILLAN AND CO., LONDON.

A TANGLED TALE. Reprinted from *The Monthly Packet*. With Six Illustrations by ARTHUR B. FROST. (First published in 1885.) Crown 8vo, cloth, gilt edges, 4s. 6d. Third Thousand.

THE GAME OF LOGIC. (With an Envelope containing a card diagram and nine counters—four red and five grey.) Crown 8vo, cloth, price 3s.
N.B.—The Envelope, etc., may be had separately at 3d. each.

ALICE'S ADVENTURES UNDER GROUND. Being a Facsimile of the original MS. Book, afterwards developed into "Alice's Adventures in Wonderland." With Thirty-seven Illustrations by the Author. Crown 8vo, cloth, gilt edges. 4s.

THE NURSERY ALICE. A selection of twenty of the pictures in "Alice's Adventures in Wonderland," enlarged and coloured under the Artist's superintendence, with explanations. [*In preparation.*

N.B. In selling the above-mentioned books to the Trade, Messrs. Macmillan and Co. will abate 2d. in the shilling (no odd copies), and allow 5 per cent. discount for payment within six months, and 10 per cent. for cash. In selling them to the Public (for cash only) they will allow 10 per cent. discount.

MR. LEWIS CARROLL, having been requested to allow "AN EASTER GREETING" (a leaflet, addressed to children, first published in 1876, and frequently given with his books) to be sold separately, has arranged with Messrs. Harrison, of 59, Pall Mall, who will supply a single copy for 1d., or 12 for 9d., or 100 for 5s.